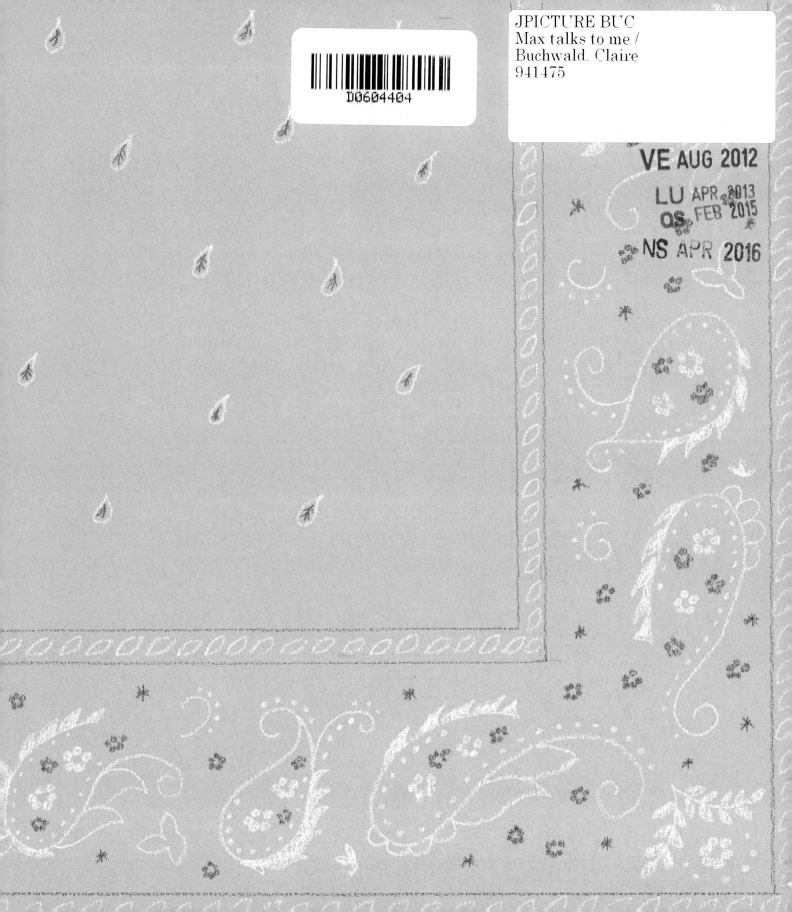

The Gryphon Press

–a voice for the voiceless–

To my parents, sisters, brothers, nephew, nieces,
husband, and children—dog lovers all—
and to the great dog loves of my life (so far):
Buck, Lyra, Lance, Foxy, Vanilla, Keltie, and Lily
—C.B.

Text design by Connie Kuhnz
Text set in Century Old Style by Prism Publication Services
Manufactured in Canada by Friesens Corporation

Library of Congress Control Number: 2006939843

ISBN-10: 0-940719-03-7
ISBN-13: 978-0-940719-03-3

1 3 5 7 9 10 8 6 4 2

A portion of profits from this book will be
donated to shelters and animal rescue societies.

I am the voice of the voiceless:
Through me, the dumb shall speak;
Till the deaf world's ear be made to hear
The cry of the wordless weak.
—from a poem by Ella Wheeler Wilcox, early 20th-century poet

Max can't speak in words,
　　　　but he does talk to me.

When I watch and listen to Max,
　　　　I know what he wants to tell me.

Max Talks to Me
Claire Buchwald • Karen Ritz

Every morning, Max tells me when it's time to get up.
He puts his front paws on the bed
and breathes hot doggy breath on my face.
Sometimes, he even tries to pull my covers off!

Max lets me know when he's hungry.
He sits by his empty dish
and looks at me.

When Max pants, I know he needs a drink.
I check to make sure he has fresh water.

When I get his leash, Max knows we're going out.
His ears are up.
His tail is high.

Sometimes, he barks or runs in circles,
as if to say,
"Yes! Yes!
We're going!"

When we're on a walk,
    Max will sniff all over.
He can smell everything much better than I can.

I bet he can smell what's cooking down the street,
    or what dog walked here before we did.
Who can tell what else he can figure out
    with just his nose?

Max watches a caterpillar move
along a blade of grass.

He sits perfectly still,
but energy zooms out of him.

I can see that any second he could play or pounce.

In the park, I throw a Frisbee, and Max catches it before it lands.

He prances around with the Frisbee
in his mouth.

I can tell he is proud of himself.

Max gets excited along with me.

When I flew a new dragon kite,
he was as happy as I was.

When the wind caught the kite,
he started barking for both of us.

Sometimes, Max and I are loud together.

We play ball or pirates.

Sometimes, we just lie in the grass and look up at the clouds.

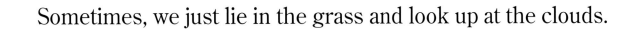

Max knows when I am sad.

When the big kids wouldn't let me hang out with them,
I sat on the steps with Max.

With his brown eyes, he looked into my sadness.

I curled my fingers into his fur,
    and some of the sadness went away.

If someone comes close to our door,
   Max tells us right away.
      His barking keeps us safe.

On the nights when we have a sitter
   so that Mom and Dad can go out,
Max lifts his head to listen for their return.

He looks the way I feel,
just waiting.

We like to curl up on the couch.

Max makes rumbling sounds in his throat
when I pet behind his ears.

Max likes it when I say, "Good dog!"
When I'm with Max, I feel good about myself.

I know he loves me completely.

I want to make Max happy, too,
so I watch him and listen to him,
because real friends
listen to each other.

Pets and Child Development

There is nothing more important parents can teach their children than empathy, caring, and the ability to communicate well. Pets can be wonderful allies in teaching these crucial skills. Pets give love unselfishly. Teaching children to pick up on pets' signals, to give love back and to attend to pets' needs is not only good pet ownership but also good parenting.

Children learn by example and by doing. You can teach your child how to pay attention to the family pet by doing so yourself and by giving your child opportunities to fulfill a pet's needs (filling a water or food dish, letting the dog in or out, petting or grooming the animal). You can also help your child be attuned to the animal by asking good questions: What do you think he is trying to tell you by whining and looking at you like that? Do you think she is happy right now? How can you tell? If you were a dog, how would you most like to be greeted when your family comes home?

Dogs Naturally Make Noise

Almost all dogs bark. Explain to your child that barking is one way that dogs "talk." When your dog barks, it is to deliver a message that can vary greatly. The dog may be saying that someone is approaching, or warning someone to back off. A bark can be an invitation to play, or to show happiness or unhappiness. Make a game of "Why Is That Dog Barking?" as a way of understanding a dog's state of mind. Other dog noises to attend to include whining or whimpering, growling, and appreciative noises such as those dogs make when being petted. As good listeners, you and your child will be able to tell at any moment if your dog is in pain, afraid, aggressive, defensive, excited, or happy. You can extend that game to others, including humans, asking your child, "Why is that person crying (or frowning or sitting far away from everyone else, etc.)?"

Smell Is a Dog's Strongest Sense

A dog's sense of smell is so keen that she can tell by sniffing an area who has passed that way over the last several hours, days, or sometimes even weeks. In fact, dogs have more than 220 million smell receptors, while humans have only 5 million. Because smell is so important to dogs, they need to be able to stop to sniff on walks to find out "what's new," just as you enjoy looking around your neighborhood. You can imagine with your child what a dog may be able to tell when he sniffs along your street.

"Listening" to Dogs Can Make Our Own Lives Better

When people and dogs pay attention to one another's signals, they can take good care of each other. A dog really can be a person's best friend: the one, who, like Max in this story, waits with you, shares your excitement, comforts you, and gives you joy.

Useful Links

Dogs and Kids: http://www.loveyourdog.com/yourbestfriend.html
Dog Communication: http://www.doggonesafe.com/dog%20communication.htm

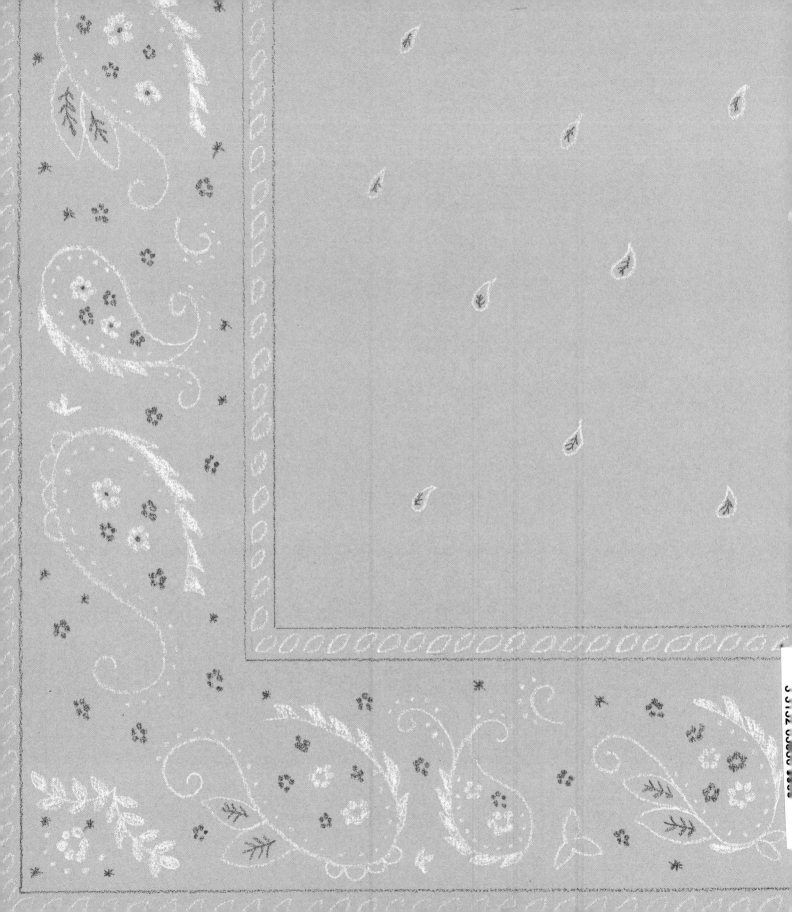